D0598146

Where's the Party?

Katharine Crawford Robey
Illustrated by Kate Endle

ini Charlesbridge

Birdsong.

Kate opens her eyes and peers outside. A robin is looking right at her. He's trying to tell her something. Kate listens hard.

"**Cheerily,**" he sings. "**News!**"
What news? Kate wants to know.
A cardinal whistles, "**Par-ty! Par-ty! Par-ty!**"
A party! Kate wants to go.

She pulls on her cowboy boots and takes the stairs by twos. In the kitchen Mama is making wild strawberry jam. "Where are you going in such a hurry?" she asks.

Kate stops. Where's the party? She doesn't know.

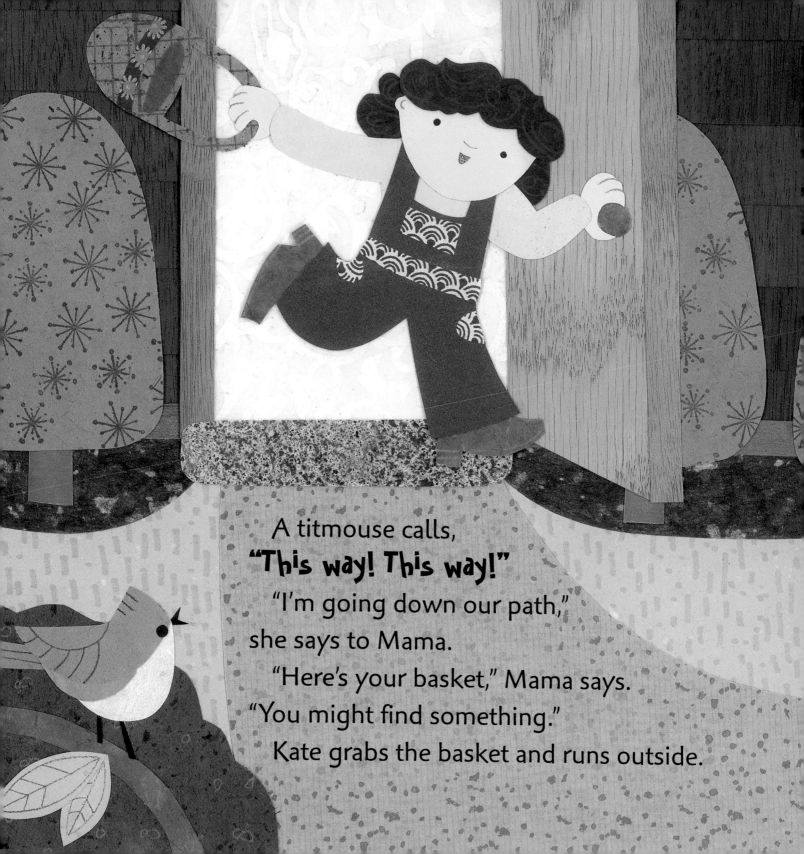

A titmouse calls,
"This way! This way!"
"I'm going down our path,"
she says to Mama.
"Here's your basket," Mama says.
"You might find something."
Kate grabs the basket and runs outside.

Daddy is hoeing in the garden. "Back soon," she tells him. He smiles and plops his visor on her head.

Kate hurries along the path. A meadowlark lands on a post nearby. His feathers look like party clothes. The meadowlark bursts out, **"Party is ne-ar! Party is ne-ar!"**

She's close. Kate looks around for the party.
Where is it?

A yellowthroat calls, **"In this tree! In this tree!"**
The bird wears a black party mask. He flies to the
apple tree. The party must be near there.

Kate runs to the tree. White blossoms lie on the ground like a fancy tablecloth. But no one is there.

An oriole swoops down. He grabs a wild strawberry in his beak and flies away without telling Kate where to go.

Kate wants strawberries, too. So red, so little,
so sweet—mmm. She puts some in her basket.

A bluebird flits up to a branch, whistling and chattering. Kate can't make out the words to his song. The bluebird gurgles like a brook. Brook! That's where she should go.

She rushes down the path. A huge bird with long legs sails up.

"Late!" croaks the great blue heron. **"Late!"**

Kate runs past marsh marigolds. She passes buzzing dragonflies and droning bees. The path ends by the big rock next to the brook.

Kate stops. There's no party here.
She sits down on the rock and lowers the visor
over her eyes. Maybe she will never find it.

A killdeer cries, "Quick, here! Quick, here!"

Where? Kate doesn't know. Just then, the reeds part. A big mallard duck appears. He struts to the brook with his chest puffed out. What is he so proud of?

Kate hops across the brook and peers through the long grass. Something is hidden there—a large nest of weeds and feathers. Tiny brown-and-yellow ducklings peek out from under their mother. They make an excited racket. **"Peep, peep!"**

No wonder Father Duck is proud. It's a birthday party for ducklings! The birds have sung her to it. It's right here, at the nest.

"Week, week, week!" peep the ducklings.
Kate tries to figure it out. The ducklings peep again.
That's it! The babies are a whole week old.

Kate's come without a present. What to do?
"Think! Think! Think!" quacks Mother from the nest.
Kate remembers the basket. She has a present after
all—wild strawberries for wild ducklings.

Slowly, quietly, she empties her basket near the rim of the nest. Mother Duck lets her babies gobble them up.

"Thanks! Thanks! Thanks!" she quacks.

Kate smiles wide and watches the ducklings.
The ducklings watch Kate, too. They look soft
and fluffy. She reaches out to touch one.

Father Duck waddles up and shakes his wet tail
feathers. Mother Duck stretches her neck out at Kate.
"Hiss!"

Kate gets the hint. The party is over. She takes one last look at the ducklings and backs away. She's glad she was able to come.

Kate takes the path from the brook, past the apple tree to her yard, back to Daddy. She is hungry.

"What's in your basket?" Daddy says.

She plops his visor back on his head. "Nothing, Daddy," she says. She turns the basket upside down and smiles. She has a secret.

Mama comes outside. "Toast and wild jam for breakfast."

"**Par-ty! Par-ty! Par-ty!**" whistles the cardinal.

Glossary of Birds in the Story

The **American robin** (*Turdus migratorius*) is familiar to most people. It is medium-sized with a rust-colored breast and gray back. Robins like to bow as they hunt for worms in yards and parks. They make cup-shaped nests from mud and grass. Robins live throughout the United States. A robin carols out, "Cheer-ee, cheer-up."

The **northern cardinal** (*Cardinalis cardinalis*) is a little smaller than the robin. It wears a fan of feathers on its head called a crest. The male is all red, except for black around its beak. The female is peachy brown. Cardinals are common in the East and in parts of the Southwest. Cardinals make all sorts of clear whistle calls, like "Thew, thew, thew, purdy, purdy, purdy" or "Cheer, cheer, cheer."

The **tufted titmouse** (*Baeolophus bicolor*) is a small gray bird with a creamy breast and tuft, or crest. This bird could fit in the palm of your hand. The titmouse likes to visit bird feeders. It holds food with its feet and pecks at it. The tufted titmouse has soft whistled calls that sound like "Peter, Peter, Peter" or "Phew, phew, phew."

The **eastern meadowlark** (*Sturnella magna*) is a medium-sized bird of the fields. It has a brown back and a bright yellow breast with a black feather V under its chin. Meadowlarks build their nests on the ground. They weave a grass roof on top. To some people, the eastern meadowlark's whistled call sounds like "Spring of the ye-ar!"

The **common yellowthroat** (*Geothlypis trichas*) is a small warbler that nests in damp spots and marshes. The yellowthroat has a bright yellow breast and a black feather mask over its eyes. Its song is a rolling warble: "Witchety-witchety-witchety."

The **Baltimore oriole** (*Icterus galbula*) is a little smaller than a robin. The male's breast feathers are bright, almost neon orange. The Baltimore oriole lives in the East, but there are other types of orioles in the West. Baltimore orioles weave a hanging nest. They have a beautiful song full of whistles and chatters.

The **eastern bluebird** (*Sialia sialis*) is one of our most beloved birds. Its back is blue as the sky, and its breast has rusty orange on it. Bluebirds like to nest in birdhouses. Their song is made up of short, sweet warbles.

The **great blue heron** (*Ardea herodias*) is a huge bird that likes to spear fish in the water with its bill. The heron looks more gray than blue, except when its feathers are caught in the sunlight. Herons make low, guttural croaks. They live throughout the United States.

The **killdeer** (*Charadrius vociferus*) is a big plover with the noisy cry, "Kill deer! Kill deer!" You might see the killdeer flying over fields or even walking along airport runways. Killdeers lay their eggs on the bare ground. They can be found throughout the United States.

The **mallard** (*Anas platyrhynchos*) is our most familiar duck. The male has a bright green head and orange feet. You can often see mallards in ponds. Their ducklings are yellow and brown. Mallards make noisy quacks like barnyard ducks.

Resources

Cornell Lab of Ornithology. "All About Birds." www.birds.cornell.edu.

Peterson Field Guide to Birds of North America. Boston: Houghton Mifflin Harcourt, 2008.

Stokes, Donald, and Lillian Stokes. *Stokes Beginner's Guide to Birds: Eastern Region.* Boston: Little, Brown, 1996.

Stokes, Donald, and Lillian Stokes. *Stokes Beginner's Guide to Birds: Western Region.* Boston: Little, Brown, 1996.

Stokes, Donald, and Lillian Stokes. *Stokes Field Guide to Bird Songs: Eastern Region.* Time Warner AudioBooks, 1997.

For my husband, Ronald, who made it possible—K. C. R.

To Chris Ballew, my favorite bird watching companion—K. E.

Text copyright © 2011 by Katharine Crawford Robey
Illustrations copyright © 2011 by Kate Endle

Published by Charlesbridge
85 Main Street
Watertown, MA 02472
(617) 926-0329
www.charlesbridge.com

Library of Congress Cataloging-in-Publication Data
Robey, Katharine.
    Where's the party? / Katharine Crawford Robey ; illustrated by Kate Endle.
        p. cm.
    Summary: A great variety of birds, with their different songs, invite Kate
to a party to celebrate some new ducklings. Includes facts about
the birds mentioned in the story.
Summary: Includes bibliographical references.
ISBN 978-1-58089-268-1 (reinforced for library use)
ISBN 978-1-58089-269-8 (softcover)
[1. Birds—Fiction. 2. Birdsongs—Fiction.] I. Endle, Kate, ill.
II. Title.
PZ7.R55175Wh 2011
[E]—dc22   2010023551

Printed in Singapore
(hc) 10 9 8 7 6 5 4 3 2 1
(sc) 10 9 8 7 6 5 4 3 2 1

Illustrations created with mixed media collage and adhered to
    300-lb. Arches cold-press watercolor paper
Display type and text type set in Big Limbo BT and
    Palatino Sans Informal LT Pro
Color separations by Chroma Graphics, Singapore
Printed and bound February 2011 by Imago in Singapore
Production supervision by Brian G. Walker
Designed by Martha MacLeod Sikkema